Sleepover Duck!

xz
B

Carin Bramsen

Random House 🏠 New York

Hey, Cat! My mom said it's all right to sleep inside the barn tonight.

A slumber party here with me?

We'll have a slumber

JAMBOREEEEE!

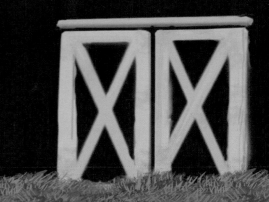

It's nice and quiet
here in back.

**A *sleepover*.
I'm all a-quack.**

Yippeeee!

**We finally get a chance
to do the slumber party dance!**

Now let the slumber games begin. . . .

Whoever sleeps is OUT!

Zzzzzzz . . .

You win.

HEY, CAT!

Must we nod off right now?
Alas, I've just forgotten how.

Well, lie down first. Try breathing deep.
It's not so hard to fall asleep.

Then I'll lie here, if you don't mind.
Oh, thanks. That's better. You're too kind.
My friend, this party is a ball.

Woo-hoooo!

Was that a party call?

Hey, Cat! Let's see if that **woo-hoo** means someone wants to party, too.

Okay, but let's not wake the house. . . .

I'll be as quiet as a mouse.

Excuse me, did you say **woo-hoo**?

No, dear. I normally say **moooo**.

Hello! Was that *your* party cry?

No, I just whispered, "Hush-a-bye."

Did you call out woo-hoo, Ms. Sheep?

No, hon. I'm counting down to sleep.

Ms. Sow's asleep.
Her piglets, too.

So where's the one
who said **woo-hoo**?

I think that we've
looked everywhere.

**Let's search the hayloft,
way up there!**

Duck, have you found
who said **woo-hoo**?

Aha. I see it's time to rest.
Sweet dreams to you, my duckie guest.

Yooo-hooooo!

Why did you close your eyes?
I thought this was a party, guys.

Why, *that's* the voice that said **woo-hoo**!
The secret party guest is *you*!

How do you dooooo? Owlette's my name,
and hide-and-seek's my favorite game.

This party night
has been the best!

But maybe now
you'd like to rest.

My friends, till next time.
Toodle-ooooo!

Good night, Owlette.
Great meeting you!

You do seem kind of sleepy, Cat.
But I just say **woo-hoo** to that!

There's nothing I would rather do
than get all tuckered out with you.